THE UNEXPLAINED

THE UNEXPLAINED

THE PYRAMID INCIDENT

TERRANCE DICKS

PICCADILLY PRESS • LONDON

This edition published 2009
First published in Great Britain in 1999
by Piccadilly Press Ltd,
5 Castle Road, London NW1 8PR
www.piccadillypress.co.uk

A catalogue record for this book is available from the British Library

ISBN: 978 1 84812 032 7 (paperback)

1 3 5 7 9 10 8 6 4 2

Printed and bound in Great Britain by CPI Bookmarque Ltd
Cover design by Patrick Knowles
Cover illustration by John Avon

Prologue

Zaki was robbing a tomb.

In his long black robes and black headcloth he was almost invisible in the desert night. His shaded lantern showed only the tiniest gleam of light. He worked swiftly and silently, clearing away the last of the sand with his bare hands.

Such efficiency was only to be expected. Tomb-robbing was Zaki's profession. As a matter of fact, it was the family business. His father, his grandfather, and even his great-grandfather had all been tomb-robbers before him.

It was the hard work of his ancestors, and others like them, that made life so difficult for Zaki now. All known tombs had been looted long ago. There was simply nothing left to steal.

To make real money, the big haul of which he had always dreamed, Zaki knew he must find a still untouched tomb.

There had long been vague but persistent rumours of an undiscovered tomb somewhere in the desert. It was rumoured that its location was known to a set of fanatical terrorists, who guarded the secret jealously.

Zaki had made friends with a minor member of the gang, plied him with forbidden drink, and learned, not the exact location of the tomb, but at least the general area – an oasis in the Eastern Desert.

His patient search had taken him to an isolated group of sand dunes, deep in the desert. Something about one of them aroused his curiosity. It seemed too neat, somehow, almost man-made. And if that was the case – what did the sand dune hide?

After hours of solitary labour Zaki had found the answer.

It hid a pyramid. Smaller than most, admittedly, but still – an entire pyramid, untouched for thousands of years!

Zaki had a feeling that this pyramid had been deliberately concealed. What treasures it must hold!

His patient work had cleared the sand and rubble from the pyramid's tip. Now, listening intently, Zaki tapped the side of the pyramid with his hammer. The sound rang hollow.

Zaki nodded in satisfaction. The pyramid would be honeycombed with passages, leading to a central burial chamber. What would he find there? A solid gold coffin, perhaps, decorated with precious jewels . . .

But first he must break in. Swinging the hammer, he struck the side of the pyramid again and again. Astonishingly, his blows had no result. The hammer rebounded from the surface of the pyramid without leaving a mark.

He raised the hammer to strike again but, to his

amazement, a narrow door slid silently open before him. Zaki raised his lantern. It revealed a passage sloping steeply downwards. He hesitated just for a moment, then greed overcame his fear.

He went inside, following the passage down into the heart of the pyramid.

Minutes went by . . .

Suddenly the doorway in the pyramid blazed with a fiercely-burning light. The silence of the desert was shattered by a terrible scream.

Zaki hurtled out of the doorway. He ran across the desert sands with incredible speed, almost as if the pyramid had somehow expelled him, shot him out like a cannonball.

His black robes were on fire and his entire body glowed.

Still screaming, Zaki sped across the valley like a human comet and disappeared from view.

The door in the pyramid closed.

After a moment the desert shuddered – as if experiencing a minor earthquake. The sand flowed smoothly up the sides of the pyramid, obliterating

The Pyramid Incident

Zaki's work and concealing the pyramid once more.

The dust settled, and the desert returned to its age-old silence.

Chapter One

EGYPT

Dad stared up at the camel.

The camel stared back down at him. It was wearing an ornate headband decorated with bobbles of multi-coloured rope, and looked, I thought, like an elderly spinster trying to look cool.

The two of them glared unblinkingly at each other.

They were extraordinarily alike to my mind – both arrogant, irritable, and contemptuous of all they surveyed.

The camel driver meanwhile carried on singing the animal's praises.

'A prince among camels, *Effendi*, as is fitting for such a great one as yourself. To ride on his back is to float on a magic carpet . . .'

'No doubt,' said Dad acidly. 'But no thank you all the same.' He sneered at the camel, the camel wrinkled its lip – and I shoved Dad aside just in time.

A substantial gob of camel spit whizzed past his head and sizzled into the sand at our feet.

Giving up, the camel driver muttered something in Arabic – it may have been a blessing, but I doubt it – and led the disdainful beast away.

Dad, meanwhile, was recovering his balance – and his dignity. 'Thank you, Matthew. How did you know about that animal's disgusting habits?'

'I read up on camels before we came. That's how they express their displeasure. That and kicking you.'

Dad sighed. 'You know, I'm beginning to think this trip was a mistake. It's hard to appreciate the glories of the past when the more unpleasant side of the present is crowding in on you.'

The Pyramid Incident

We were in Egypt, on the Giza Plateau just outside Cairo.

The Sphinx and the Giza Pyramids were just as magnificent as they were in all the photographs I'd seen. But what hadn't got into the photographs was the hot and dusty desert area around them. It was a mixture of tatty suburbs on one side, a bazaar and a building-site on the other two sides with the desert housing the pyramids and stretching for miles.

It was littered with bits of fencing and unfinished constructions guarded with straggling barbed wire.

It was swarming with licensed and unlicensed tour guides, would-be horse and camel drivers, refreshment and souvenir sellers, and very persistent pedlars, beggars and hawkers of every kind. There were also surprising numbers of grim-faced armed police.

Then there were our fellow tourists – by the bus-load. Not quite as many as usual this year. Recent terrorist activity had kept quite a few of them away.

The shortage made every hotel tout, tour guide and hawker more determined than usual to gather what *baksheesh* they could from those tourists who *had* turned up. Which included us.

You couldn't really blame them: Egypt depends heavily on tourism. *Baksheesh* means 'share the wealth', and compared to the average tourist most of these people were desperately poor. But being bombarded with constant sales pitches made for a pretty stressful time.

It was hot, noisy and crowded – three of the things Dad dislikes most. I was doing my best to keep cheerful, but I was rapidly coming to share Dad's sentiments.

We'd been in Egypt for several days now, and I was beginning to wonder if the trip was such a good idea after all.

To make matters worse, it was my fault we were here . . .

I'm Matthew Stirling.

Dad is Professor James Stirling, leading space scientist and all-round egghead.

Although we're father and son, we're still getting to know each other. My parents split up when I was still a baby and Dad went off to work in America. Mum brought me up at first – until she was killed in a road accident. Then an uncle and aunt took over.

When they retired and went to live abroad, Dad suddenly found himself stuck with hitherto neglected parental responsibilities, in the overgrown shape of a teenage son. Me!

He was hit by another crisis at the same point, this time a professional one. Funds for his space-research project suddenly dried up, and he found himself out of work. Luckily there was a top job on offer – Director of Paranormal Studies for a big American scientific research institute.

Always a man for the dynamic decision, Dad solved both his problems at a stroke. He took the paranormal studies job – even though he felt it was a bit of a come-down for a sceptical, no-nonsense scientist – and made me his assistant.

He also took me out of school, loftily declaring that he'd see to my education himself, at least until I was old enough for university. Since he's got degrees in everything you can think of, nobody dared argue.

Indirectly speaking, it was this last decision that landed us in Egypt.

Since I'd become Dad's assistant we'd visited quite a few exotic spots around the world investigating reports of paranormal activity. Some proved to be no more than imaginary bogeymen. Others had more to them, and we'd encountered some very strange and inexplicable events.

Egypt was supposed to be different. No spooks, nothing weird, just mind-broadening educational travel.

It had all started one evening during one of our not-infrequent dust-ups. Dad had been grumbling about my lack of dedication to my studies. I retaliated by complaining that his idea of education was all work and no play.

'Look at all the stuff I'm missing out on,' I said. 'There was a trip to Egypt coming up when you took me out of school. How can I grow up into a fully-rounded individual if I don't get a balanced education?'

'You can scarcely complain of a lack of travel,'

snapped Dad. 'Considering that we've recently visited Australia, America and Easter Island . . .'

'That was work,' I objected. 'You don't get much time for taking in the local culture when you're chasing around the Australian outback hunting aliens.'

We'd found them too, I was sure of it – by the Sacred Rock of the Aborigines. I think I felt an alien presence there – something in my mind, like they were trying to communicate in thought, but I couldn't be sure. Dad was though. He reckoned it was a load of rubbish.

Our conversation didn't seem to make much impression on Dad at the time. He's an obstinate old devil and hates to admit he could be wrong about any-thing. All the same, more must've sunk in than I thought.

A few days later I was idly surfing the internet when a fat folder of travel documents landed on the desk in front of me.

I looked up. 'What's all this?'

'Tickets for a tour of Egypt,' said Dad. 'We leave

for Cairo tomorrow. Heaven forbid that you should suffer from an unbalanced education!'

Typical!

But I couldn't complain. After all, I'd brought it on myself. Though I was worried all the same. Facing the unknown dangers of the paranormal is frightening enough, but a family holiday with Dad? That's really scary.

Dad had booked us a luxury, personally-tailored tour with one of the posher travel agencies. We were staying at the multi-storeyed Nile Splendide, which was exactly like other luxury hotels all over the world. We had a two-bedroom suite with a terrific view of the Nile.

So far so good. It was when the holiday really got going that the trouble started.

The Nile Splendide is on Midan Tahrir, a big square in central Cairo, close to the Egyptian Museum.

Guess where we spent all of the first few days of our holiday?

The Egyptian Museum is enormous. Huge, old-fashioned and shambolic, it contains over one hundred thousand relics of Egyptian antiquity, and I'll swear we saw nearly all of them.

The Tutankhamun Galleries alone hold about one thousand seven hundred items, nearly all priceless. There are gold and jewelled amulets, alabaster jars and caskets, gold sandals, a gold bed, and a gold face-mask of Tutankhamun himself.

After a couple of days of museum trudging I'd rebelled. 'I'd like to see a bit of Ancient Egypt that isn't in a glass case,' I'd said.

Dad had grumbled a bit, but eventually agreed that it was time we saw the pyramids . . .

So, here we were on the Giza Plateau: hot, dusty and tired, being pestered by hawkers and soft-drink sellers and spat at by camels.

Once you're in Cairo, the pyramids are on your doorstep. All we'd had to do to see them was to catch the minibus from outside the hotel.

We'd visited the largest already – the Great Pyramid of Cheops – and had climbed through the maze of narrow passages inside.

The Unexplained

We'd studied the Sphinx, the huge statue carved from a single chunk of rock. It had the body of a lion and the head of an Egyptian pharaoh. The poor old thing looked pretty fed up – not surprising, really. Napoleon's soldiers were meant to have used it for artillery practice and shot off its nose.

Now we were starting to think that we'd had enough. Even Dad admitted it.

'I think it's time we left, Matthew. Thoughts of a cool drink on the hotel terrace are beginning to out-weigh all the delights of antiquity.'

'Quite right,' I said. 'We don't want to risk cultural overload.'

We started making our way back to the minibus.

It was then that I saw the shabby little man.

He was scruffy and unshaven in a crumpled white suit and a fez. He looked like one of the hotel touts who hang around stations and airports, pretending to be official guides.

I noticed him because he looked terrified, and because he seemed to be making his way determinedly towards us.

The Pyramid Incident

I watched as he dodged around the horses and camels, the tourists and hawkers, and staggered right up to Dad, staring at him in a kind of desperate appeal.

Dad frowned down at him.

Suddenly the little man slumped forward, clutching at Dad for support.

I'm ashamed to say my first thought was that he was an exceptionally enterprising pickpocket.

Dad must have had the same idea. He jumped back, feeling instinctively for his wallet.

The little man fell face-down at our feet.

It was then I saw the dark spreading stain between his shoulder blades.

Chapter Two

The Scarab of Ra

Dad kneeled down beside the man and felt for the pulse in his neck. It was pretty clear from the look on his face that there wasn't one.

After a moment he stood up. 'He's dead.'

I was ready to take Dad's word for it. He's got a medical degree along with all the others.

By now a noisy, chattering crowd was gathering around the body.

Dad looked round. 'We must find a policeman.'

I had my own ideas about that. 'If we stay here a policeman will find us,' I said. 'There are plenty in the crowd.' I grabbed Dad's arm and drew him away from the body, allowing the curious crowd to surge forward in our place. 'I think we ought to get away from here.'

Dad was shocked. 'We can't do that, Matthew, it would be quite irresponsible.'

'It's being responsible that worries me,' I said.

'I don't understand. It's our duty to inform the police.'

'Inform them of what?' I asked. 'That there's a dead body? They can see that for themselves.'

'But, Matthew . . .'

I led him away through the crowd. 'Do you know who the dead man was?'

'Well, no, but . . .'

'Do you know who killed him?'

'Certainly not!'

'And do you know why he picked you of all people to fall down dead in front of?'

'Of course not. To the best of my knowledge I've

never seen him before.'

As Dad spoke, I suddenly realised that I felt sure I *had* seen him before. There was something about the dead man that was faintly familiar. But the feeling was too vague to pin down, and it didn't seem the moment to go into it.

I went on with my argument. 'There you are then. There's nothing useful we can tell the police.'

'Even so, Matthew . . .'

'One last question,' I said. 'How likely is it that the police will believe we don't know anything? The dead man was clearly making for us – for you. They're bound to think we're involved with him somehow, that we're hiding something. At best we'll be kept hanging about here for hours, in all this heat. We'll spend hours more waiting to make a statement in some stuffy police station.' I paused impressively. 'At worst, we'll end up in a prison cell.'

'That's ridiculous, Matthew!'

'Is it? We're not at home now, you know. The old innocent-until-proved-guilty routine doesn't necessarily apply. If the police here are suspicious they probably just lock you up for a bit until they get things sorted out. It makes life a lot simpler for them.'

Dad hesitated. 'I'm still not sure . . .'

By now we'd reached the area where the hotel buses parked. The minibus for the Nile Splendide was about to leave.

'If you really think it's necessary, we can contact the authorities later,' I said. 'But I suggest we see the British consul first and get advice.' I pointed towards the minibus. 'Well, what's it to be? Civic duty or that long cool drink?'

'My conscience still tells me we ought to stay,' said Dad. 'However, the rest of me seems to be on your side. Come on!'

We hurried towards the bus.

As we jolted back to the hotel I felt relieved and worried at the same time. Relieved because we'd avoided the clutches of the law, at least for the moment. Worried because I still didn't know what was going on.

Why had the dying man headed so determinedly for Dad? Was it simply coincidence? Or was there something much more sinister involved?

And where had I seen him before?

We discussed the morning's events over lunch and several cool drinks on the hotel terrace.

'I thought he was trying to rob you at first,' I said.

'So did I,' said Dad. Automatically, he patted his pockets. 'Nothing's gone though.' He paused. 'As a matter of fact . . .'

'What is it?'

He took his hand out of his jacket pocket. 'Rather than trying to rob me, he seems to have given me something.'

He held out his hand. On it lay a strange oval object, about half the size of a man's hand. It looked like some kind of beetle and it appeared to be made of solid gold.

Its eyes glowed ruby-red.

'It's a scarab,' said Dad. 'In other words, the Egyptian dung-beetle. Sacred to the Ancient Egyptians as the symbol of the sun-god, Ra.'

I took the object from his hand and examined it.

Fine lines and raised dots were etched on its back in some kind of design. It reminded me of the veins on the back of a leaf.

A tiny diamond glinted amongst them.

'Is it genuine?' I asked. 'Genuine Ancient Egyptian, I mean. It looks . . . well, brand new.'

Dad took the beetle back. 'Yes it does, doesn't it? Of course, if it came from some newly discovered tomb hoard . . .'

'Are there any left?'

'I wouldn't have thought so. But the desert is vast. And after all, they'd been robbing tombs for hundreds, even thousands, of years before Howard Carter found the still-untouched treasure of Tutankhamun.'

He fished out a magnifying lens and studied the scarab more closely. 'I've never seen anything like these markings before. And why this single diamond on the back?'

After a moment he put the lens away and looked up. 'I'm afraid I'm not enough of an expert to say if it's genuine or a reproduction. We could take it to somebody at the museum.'

'Then we'd have to tell him or her where we got it,' I said. 'That could be rather awkward.'

'Why should it? We can simply explain . . .'

'That it was a present from a dead man?' I shook my head. 'Now that this thing's turned up the police will be sure we're involved in some way. They might even think we killed him to get our hands on it.'

We stared at the beetle in mutual puzzlement.

'Why did he want you to have it?' I wondered aloud.

Dad shrugged. 'Who knows? We don't even know who he was.'

I told Dad about my feeling that I'd seen the dead man before.

He leaned forward eagerly. 'Where, Matthew? When? This is vitally important. If there really is some connection between us and the dead man, it puts everything in a whole new light. Where did you see him?'

'I don't know,' I said helplessly. 'I've got a feeling it wasn't in Egypt at all, but somewhere different, a different context. You know, the way you see the man from your local shop in the street and don't recognise him, just because you've always seen him behind a counter. I've been racking my brains but it just won't come.'

'Stop racking,' ordered Dad. 'That sort of information pops out of the subconscious more easily when you don't struggle for it. We'll just have to hope something triggers your memory.'

He looked down at the jewelled scarab. 'Meanwhile, what do we do with this thing? It seems to be made of solid gold, and if that diamond on the back is genuine and those eyes are real rubies . . . Antique or modern, it must be worth a fortune.'

'For a start, don't go walking about with it in your pocket,' I said. 'Let's put it in the hotel safe while we think things over.'

After lunch Dad bought a small padded envelope and some Sellotape in the hotel shop, sealed the scarab amulet into the envelope, wrote his name on it and handed it to the hotel manager at reception.

The manager promised to put it straight into the

safe, and to hand it over to nobody but Dad in person.

'Now what?' Dad said when it was done.

'I think we had better just carry on with our planned programme,' I said. 'The more natural and touristy we act, the better.'

'Why?'

'In case we're being watched.'

The programme that afternoon was a visit to the bazaar in the old quarter of the city.

The bazaar was very much what you might expect – narrow winding streets packed with all kinds of people and lined with shops and stalls.

Cairo is one of the most densely populated cities in the world, crowded not only with Egyptians, but with Arabs, Africans and Sudanese. There is a surprising number of Europeans as well, some resident, some tourists like us.

Like the camel-hirers at the pyramids, the stall-keepers were very pushy. Pause to admire a carpet, a crystal goblet or a lamp and you were practically hauled inside the shop for a long bout of haggling. On the other hand, if you didn't stop and look at things, there didn't seem very much point in being there at all.

It was as hot, noisy and crowded as it had been on the pyramid site, and Dad and I were soon feeling frazzled again. I was beginning to go off this tourism lark altogether. If it wasn't for the mystery we seemed to be mixed up in, I might have suggested an early return home. In the baking heat, wet and windy London felt positively attractive.

But I couldn't forget the scruffy little man in the white suit, and the look of appeal in his eyes as he'd collapsed dead at our feet. And I still couldn't remember where I'd seen him before . . .

We turned into one of the quieter side streets, a narrow cul-de-sac, and sat down at a pavement café.

We'd been thinking of a cold beer for Dad and a Coke for me. Before we could say anything a wizened and ancient waiter brought us little cups of sweet black coffee.

We settled for that. It was nice to sit down anyway.

We sat sipping our coffee and watching the crowds

passing by at the end of the street.

Suddenly three men turned into the cul-de-sac. Two of them, both massive-looking, stayed at the far end.

The third walked up to our table.

He was slender and dark, hawk-faced, with a thin moustache. He wore black, flowing robes with an Arab headdress.

For a moment he stood looking down at us with burning eyes. '*Salaam 'alekum*,' he said at last.

I knew enough phrase-book Arabic to recognise this as the standard polite greeting: 'Peace be upon you.'

I made the standard polite reply. '*War 'alekum es salaam*' – 'Upon you be peace.'

'May I join you?' he said.

'If you wish,' said Dad.

The stranger pulled a chair from an adjoining table and sat at our table. Instantly the waiter scurried forward with a coffee. The stranger sipped it, studying us for a moment over the rim of the coffee cup.

'I trust you are enjoying your visit to Cairo?'

I'd read somewhere that it's the custom in the Middle East to spend ages in polite small talk before getting down to business.

Either Dad didn't know this, or he didn't care. He was never much of a diplomat. 'What can we do for you?' he asked.

The stranger said, 'You can return the Scarab of Ra.' Before Dad could say anything, he held up his hand. 'Please, do not waste time by denying possession of the scarab. I know that the thief had it in his possession when I caught up with him at the Pyramids of Giza. We know too that he passed it on to you.'

'How do you know that?'

'Because it was not upon his body – and he had contact with no one else.'

Dad considered for a moment. 'Even if what you say is correct – and I admit nothing – why should I give the scarab to you?'

'Because I am its rightful owner,' snapped the stranger.

'How can I be sure of that?' said Dad sharply. 'You accuse the dead man, who can no longer defend himself, of being a thief. Yet by your own admission you are a murderer. Perhaps the dead man was the rightful owner and you are the thief.'

The stranger's eyes blazed with anger. 'You insult me!' He regained control with an effort. 'I have neither the time nor the patience to give you proof that what I say is true. But I can give you at least one excellent reason for doing as I ask.'

'Which is?'

'Unless you return the scarab, you will both be killed.'

I'll say this for Dad, there's absolutely nothing wrong with his nerve. His only response to the threat was a contemptuous smile.

'Here and now? In the middle of a crowded bazaar?'

'Why not?' said the stranger coolly. 'This is Cairo. Nobody will see anything.' He smiled. 'At least, nobody will speak of it if they do. I am Abd al Rashid!'

He paused for a reaction and seemed disappointed when he didn't get it. 'Believe me,' he snarled, 'I have killed many Westerners in places as public as this.'

The hatred in his voice was terrifying.

I suddenly remembered recent stories of terrorist attacks. Mostly on police and security forces, but sometimes on tourists as well. Discouraging tourism was one of the terrorists' aims.

There had been bombs at the Egyptian Museum and on the road to the pyramids. A tourist boat had been machine-gunned on the Nile, and seventeen Greek tourists shot down when their coach was ambushed . . .

'Well?' said Rashid. 'Are you going to give me the scarab?'

I'd have taken him to the hotel and handed it over on the spot. Dad however, was far too pig-headed to be sensible.

'I am not in the habit of giving way to threats,' he said coldly. 'Please leave.'

For the first time Rashid turned his attention to me – attention I could have done without.

'I take it that this fine young man is your son? We prize our sons greatly in Egypt. I am sure it is the same in the West.'

Now it was Dad's turn to be angry. 'If you dare to threaten . . .'

Suddenly there was an automatic in Rashid's hand – pointed not at Dad, but at me.

'Which do you value most? The scarab, or the life of your son?'

Chapter Three

Terrorist

Dad went white and his hands gripped the edge of the table. He looked ready to jump at Rashid.

Personally, I didn't think this was any time for heroics.

'Hey, Dad,' I said urgently. 'Just remember where that gun's pointing!'

He controlled himself with a mighty effort. 'All right, Matthew, point taken.' He sat back in his chair and looked at Rashid. 'The scarab isn't here.'

'You lie! Give it to me, or I kill the boy.'

'Don't be silly,' I said calmly – or as calmly as I could manage. 'Do you think anyone would walk round a crowded bazaar with the scarab in his pocket – knowing you, or someone like you, might be after them?'

'Then where is it?'

'In the safe at our hotel,' said Dad.

'Which hotel?'

'The Nile Splendide.'

Rashid thought for a moment. 'You will write a letter ordering the scarab to be handed over to my messenger.'

Dad shook his head. 'It won't do. I left specific instructions that it was to be returned to me, and to me alone. You'll have to come back to the hotel with us.'

'And risk your escape – or my capture?' said Rashid scornfully. 'I do not think so. You will go back to the hotel, while the boy stays with us.' He nodded towards his two henchmen. 'If you do not return in an hour with the scarab, we will cut his throat.'

'No,' said Dad. 'I won't leave him in your hands.

Suppose I get run over? Suppose the manager is unavailable and there's a delay in my getting the scarab? I refuse to risk it.'

'Then we shall kill you both.'

'Then you won't get the scarab,' I said.

'We shall take it from the hotel safe!'

'You'll have a job doing that,' I said. 'Thanks to your recent activities, the hotel area is swarming with police.'

'I do not fear the police. I am Abd al Rashid!'

Rashid glared at us, angry and confused. It struck me that there was something almost childlike about his boasting – but it didn't mean that he wasn't dangerous.

He scowled at us. I could see that he was considering his options. Risk coming to the hotel? Kill us both now? Try threatening us some more?

I never found out what his decision would be.

It was at that moment that the beggar lurched into the alley. He wore a dirty striped *galabiyya*, the full-length robe worn by most ordinary Egyptians, and his head was wrapped in a scarf. He shuffled up to our table.

'*Baksheesh, Effendi, baksheesh*,' he whined. 'A few miserable piastres to save the life of a starving man . . .'

It struck me that he didn't look starving. For a beggar he was exceptionally big and burly.

Annoyed at the interruption, Rashid gestured to his two bodyguards. They came and grabbed the beggar and tried to hustle him away.

The beggar resisted wildly, and suddenly the whole struggling group fell into our table, sending the table, Dad, me and Rashid to the ground in a tangled heap.

A hand grabbed my arm and an urgent voice hissed, 'Matt, Professor – this way!'

The beggar pulled us both to our feet and hustled us into the little café. Then he picked up the iron table and hurled it at Rashid and his men, who were just getting to their feet. I heard an angry shout and then a gunshot. A bullet spanged off the iron table.

Then we were running through the dark little café and into a tiny kitchen where the wizened waiter stood stirring a cooking pot. He paid no attention to us as we ran past him and out of the back door. Maybe shoot-outs were an everyday affair in his café. Or maybe he thought it was safer not to see anything.

The back door of the kitchen led us to a tiny cluttered yard and we charged through a flock of indignant chickens and out of the back gate, which led into a narrow back alley.

'Right, follow me!' said the beggar in surprisingly good English. 'Quick as you can, they'll be after us.'

We followed the striped *galabiyya* out of the winding alley, into a crowded backstreet and then to the corner of a busy main road where a taxi stood waiting, engine running. The beggar shoved us both inside and then disappeared into the crowd.

The taxi shot off into the stream of Cairo traffic, attracting the usual shouts, yells and hoots from indignant motorists.

Bounced up and down in the jolting taxi, Dad and I looked at each other in stunned amazement.

'Good grief,' said Dad mildly. 'What an extraordinary experience! Although I'm still not actually sure if we're being rescued or kidnapped.'

* * *

We needn't have worried. The taxi screeched to a halt outside the Nile Splendide and we both got out. Dad automatically reached for his wallet, but the taxi was already roaring away.

'Even more extraordinary,' said Dad. 'A taxi driver who doesn't want paying!'

'All part of the service,' I said.

'Yes, but whose service?'

I already had a pretty good idea, and my suspicions were soon to be confirmed.

We went into the luxurious hotel foyer. After our recent experiences, it was like entering a different world. We went over to the reception desk and Dad had a word with the manager.

'The package I left with you . . .'

'Bestowed in the hotel safe as you requested, sir. Do you want it back?'

'Not for the moment.' Dad hesitated. 'I feel I should warn you that the contents of the envelope are extremely valuable. There is a distinct possibility that some attempt might be made to steal it.'

'Have no fear,' said the manager grandly. 'Our

security is excellent. The safe alarm is linked to a nearby police post. Any attempt at theft will be met by an instant response.'

I wondered how their security would stand up to the arrival of Rashid and a gang of armed terrorists, but there didn't seem to be any point in going on about it.

When we went to collect our keys the desk clerk said, 'There's a message for you, Professor Stirling.' He took an envelope from a pigeonhole and handed it over.

Dad opened the envelope and took out a single sheet of paper. He read the brief message and handed it over to me.

The message said that Ms Alexander would be obliged if we met her for a drink in the bar at six o'clock.

Ms Alexander was head of a mysterious intelligence department in London. We had been involved with her on several of our previous investigations.

We'd met her for the first time when we'd been looking at a weird series of events centred around

Stonehenge. After that, she tended to send for us whenever the supernatural seemed to be getting mixed up with security.

I nodded and handed the message back without saying anything.

Dad raised an eyebrow. 'You don't seem to be very surprised.'

'I'm not.'

'May I ask why?'

I grinned. Dad hates it when I'm a step ahead of him. 'You weren't fooled by the robes and the skin dye, were you?' I asked innocently.

Dad frowned. 'This business is quite mysterious enough, Matthew. Kindly stop talking in riddles.'

'That mysterious beggar, the one who rescued us . . .'

'What about him?'

'That was Jim Wainwright, Ms Alexander's deputy director . . .'

At a few minutes past six, Dad and I came down from our suite, showered, changed and rested. Dad collected his envelope from the hotel safe and we made our way to the bar.

We found Ms Alexander and Jim Wainwright waiting for us at a corner table. Secret agents like to sit with their backs to the wall and a good view of the room.

A waiter showed us to their table. We sat down, ordered drinks and exchanged the usual greetings. We made small talk about the heat until the drinks arrived.

Ms Alexander looked the same as ever – cool, calm and relaxed in a well-tailored linen suit and serious glasses. She looked, as always, like a woman who'd crashed through the glass ceiling and was now running a merchant bank, or a big corporation.

Jim Wainwright had swapped his *galabiyya* for a lightweight tropical suit. He'd washed off the skin dye and was back to a normal tourist tan.

'You've still got a few streaks of dye round your neck,' I said, when the waiter had gone. 'Isn't all that Lawrence of Arabia stuff a bit out of date these days?'

Jim Wainwright grinned at me. He's a large, tough,

competent man – a sort of everyday, real life James Bond.

'I'll have you know my Arabic's pretty good, Matthew. I spent several years in the Yemen with the SAS. I'm the wrong size and shape to pass for an Arab for very long, but I can get by for a bit in a minor role.'

'You played a major role in rescuing us today,' said Dad. 'I'm very grateful – things were looking ugly.'

'How on earth did you manage to turn up in the proverbial nick of time?' I asked.

Wainwright instinctively glanced at Ms Alexander, and she nodded permission.

'I was hanging about in the bazaar in my beggar disguise,' he said, 'trying to find a character called Abd al Rashid. I managed to get on his track so I followed him. To my amazement, I found he was following you two. I watched him corner you in the café and kept an eye on things. When he pulled the gun I thought it was time to intervene.'

'I'm glad you did,' I said. 'The conversation wasn't going very well.'

'Now, Professor,' said Ms Alexander sharply. 'Perhaps

you'll be good enough to tell me how you became involved with one of Egypt's leading terrorists?'

'With pleasure,' said Dad, equally sharply.

He delivered a concise account of the events at the pyramids, telling how the little man had secretly passed him the scarab and then dropped dead at his feet.

'The thing that still baffles me,' he concluded, 'is why on earth the poor fellow picked on me.'

'I can tell you that,' I said.

Dad gave me his indignant glare. 'You can? Why didn't you say so before?'

'Because I've only just realised,' I said. I looked at Wainwright and Ms Alexander. 'Seeing you two gave me the context I needed. He was one of your agents, wasn't he?'

Cautious as ever, they didn't reply.

'I saw him a couple of times at your HQ,' I said. 'When we came in for our conferences. Not to speak to or anything, he was just there. We passed in a corridor, rode up in a lift together, that sort of thing. I hardly registered him, he was such an inconspicuous little chap. I assumed he was a filing clerk or something.'

Once again Wainwright glanced at Ms Alexander, and once again she gave a little nod of consent.

'His name was Simon Carstairs,' said Wainwright. 'Being inconspicuous was one of his greatest strengths. He really could pass for an Arab – or an Indian, or a Frenchman, or anything else.'

I looked at Dad. 'Just as I noticed him, he must have noticed you. When he was on the run at the pyramids, wounded and dying with something he was desperate to get rid of, he saw you as someone he could trust and slipped you the scarab.'

'He was working for us out here,' said Ms Alexander. 'Seconded to the Egyptian Government on anti-terrorist operations. He sent back a report that he was on to something big. Something that concerned England as well as Egypt. It sounded so urgent that we came out here to help. We were too late . . .' She paused. 'This scarab, Professor Stirling . . .'

Dad handed her the packet. She opened it and took out the golden beetle, keeping it cupped in her hand.

She studied it, and shook her head. 'It must have something to do with whatever he'd discovered,' she said, 'since he was so desperate to pass it on.'

'And since Rashid is so desperate to get it back,' I said. 'That's why he nabbed us at that café. He suspected Dad had the scarab, and was ready to kill to get his hands on it.'

Ms Alexander nodded to Dad. 'I think we'd better take charge of this, if you don't mind.'

'Please do. I never want to see the thing again. It very nearly got us both killed.'

She handed the scarab to Wainwright, who put it back in the envelope and stowed the envelope away in an inside pocket.

'This is a very fortunate meeting, Professor Stirling,' said Ms Alexander. 'I tried to contact you before we left for Egypt – only to be told that you were away on holiday.' She gave him a reproachful look. 'Leaving no contact details.'

Dad obviously didn't care for her tone. 'May I remind you, Ms Alexander, that I am a free agent.'

There was a brief spark of anger in Ms Alexander's

eyes, but she controlled her temper. 'I had intended to contact you, Professor, and enlist your aid,' she said. 'Part of Carstairs's last report suggested that certain aspects of this affair come into your area and —'

'No!' interrupted Dad.

Ms Alexander gave him an angry and astonished look. 'I'm sorry, Professor?'

'No,' said Dad again. 'I am unable to assist you.'

Ms Alexander's voice was coldly furious. 'May I ask why?'

'Because Matthew and I are about to check out of this hotel and return to England – tonight, if possible. A few hours ago my son's life was threatened. I'm grateful for Mr Wainwright's help, but I refuse to subject Matthew to any more risk.'

The business with Rashid had really got to him.

'Dad,' I started.

'No, Matthew, I won't discuss it.' He turned to Ms Alexander. 'I couldn't help you even if I wished. Terrorism is your area, not mine.'

Ms Alexander made a final attempt. 'If you would allow me to explain . . .'

Dad stood up. 'I'm sorry. Come on, Matthew.'

He strode away from the table and I had no alternative but to follow him. I was half-angry, half-touched by the violence of his reaction – and I could see that it was no use arguing with him.

Not yet, anyway.

A slender Egyptian in a dark suit and the red fez worn by officials was waiting at the restaurant door. Two uniformed policemen stood nearby.

'Professor Stirling?'

'Yes?' snapped Dad.

'I am Inspector Mahmoud of the Cairo Police.'

After all the recent upset, Dad wasn't in the best of moods. 'Indeed? And what can I do for you?'

'This is Matthew Stirling, your son?'

'Yes, yes,' snapped Dad impatiently. 'Will you kindly tell me what you want?'

'I must ask you to come with me. You are both under arrest.'

Dad stared at him. 'On what charge?'

'The charge is murder.'

Chapter Four

Set-up

It's not often you see Dad speechless, but this was one of those few times. He stared at the inspector in silent astonishment.

'There is also a charge of robbery,' Inspector Mahmoud went on. 'The theft of a valuable antique Egyptian artefact.'

'And just who are we supposed to have robbed and murdered?' I asked. 'And when?' Not that I didn't have a very good idea. I was just playing for time.

'The identity of the victim is not yet known to us. He was stabbed near to the Pyramids of Giza at approximately eleven o'clock this morning. There were two people seen close to the body – then they fled from the scene.'

Dad managed to recover his voice. 'And what makes you so sure that we're the people concerned?'

'The eyewitness descriptions correspond exactly.'

'What made you come looking for us here?' I asked.

Inspector Mahmoud didn't reply.

'I don't suppose it would have been an anonymous tip-off, would it?' I went on.

Once again the inspector didn't reply – but the look on his face was answer enough.

It was easy to guess who knew we'd been close to the body at the pyramids, knew where we were staying and wanted to get us in trouble – our terrorist friend, Abd al Rashid!

I wondered about the rest of his plan. Perhaps he thought it would be easier to steal the scarab once we were in jail. Or maybe he'd attack us on the way to the police station. His main motive was to get his hands on the scarab. But we'd made a fool of him in the bazaar. From what I'd seen of him, I thought he'd be after revenge as well.

It suddenly struck me that we were in a lot of trouble. Someone as powerful and unscrupulous as Rashid could probably come up with witnesses who'd say whatever he told them to say.

As these cheerful thoughts were flashing through my mind, I heard a voice say, 'Can I be of assistance, Inspector Mahmoud?'

Ms Alexander had come across from our table, Jim Wainwright close behind her.

Inspector Mahmoud looked round in surprise. 'Ms Alexander!' He shook his head. 'I'm afraid this is police business.'

'If it concerns these two gentlemen, it's my business as well. May I ask the nature of the problem?'

'We're accused of robbery and murder,' I said quickly. 'By the Giza Pyramids at about eleven this morning.' I looked hard at her. 'It's ridiculous – we weren't anywhere near there.'

Dad gave me an astonished look, but Ms Alexander took her cue with professional skill.

'Of course you weren't. You were here with us.'

Jim Wainwright backed her up immediately. 'We've been in a conference in our suite, all day.'

Inspector Mahmoud looked astonished – and suspicious as well. 'But the information we received – the descriptions . . .'

'You know why I am here in Cairo, inspector,' said Ms Alexander. 'My department is working with your own security people, on a matter of vital importance to both our countries. We were promised the fullest co-operation from the police. You will scarcely be helping my mission by arresting two of my most valued associates.'

Inspector Mahmoud turned to Dad. 'You confirm this, Professor? You are indeed an associate of Ms Alexander's?'

Dad hesitated for a moment. 'It's true that I have acted as a consultant to her department on a number of occasions . . .'

'And you are giving me your help with this current

problem,' said Ms Alexander. 'Isn't that so, Professor?'

There was an edge of steel in her voice. It was quite clear that our much-needed alibi came with a price.

Dad knew when he was beaten. 'Yes,' he said. 'Yes I am.'

Inspector Mahmoud knew he was beaten as well, but he didn't like it any more than Dad.

'And this question of the stolen artefact,' he said. 'To be precise, a golden scarab. Do you know anything about that?'

'I can assure you,' said Dad, 'that I have no such object in my possession.'

Inspector Mahmoud looked hard at him for a moment. 'Since Ms Alexander vouches for you, I shall take no further action – for the moment,' he said. 'However I must insist that you do not leave Cairo until this matter is cleared up.'

He gave us a stiff nod of farewell and marched away, followed by his two policemen.

Dad swung round on me in a fury. 'Matthew, whatever possessed you to tell —'

'Let's go back to the table,' said Ms Alexander. 'We need to talk.'

Dad was still fuming when we sat back down at the table. 'You've all put me in an intolerable position,' he said. 'I've committed no crime – but I've lied to the police!'

'We were facing a false accusation,' I said. 'The only way to block it was with a fake alibi.'

I told them of my suspicion that Rashid was behind things.

'Matthew's quite right, Professor,' said Jim Wainwright when I'd finished. 'It's possible that Rashid has sympathisers in the police, maybe in the legal system as well. You couldn't be sure of getting a fair trial. He'll send a dozen witnesses to court to say they actually saw you stab poor Carstairs in the back!'

Dad was silent for a moment. He turned to Ms Alexander. 'And I take it I'm obliged to pay for this false testimony with my services?'

She touched his arm. 'I'm sorry, Professor, I really am. But all's fair in love, war and security work. And

I really do need your help.'

'But why exactly?' asked Dad explosively. 'Counter-terrorism is your job, not mine. I'm not trained for it, I know nothing about it. I'm prepared to tackle the paranormal – but murderous fanatics with guns are a very different matter.'

Ms Alexander waited until the outburst was over. 'I'm not asking you to tackle terrorism,' she said quietly. 'I want you to investigate the curse of Tutankhamun.'

Chapter Five

Tutankhamun's Curse

We continued the discussion over an excellent dinner in the hotel restaurant – which did a lot to restore Dad's temper. As in most luxury hotel chains, the menu featured standard international as well as local cuisine.

Dad and I stuck to the familiar steak and chips. Ms Alexander and Wainwright, both old Cairo hands, had a variety of Egyptian dishes including *mezzes*, an assortment of vegetables, and *hammam mashwi*, which turned out to be grilled pigeon.

Ms Alexander ate two of them and Jim Wainwright had six. 'Not an awful lot on a pigeon,' he said apologetically. 'And I'm a growing lad!'

Several glasses of a local red wine called Omar Khayam also helped to put Dad in a better mood.

When the meal was over and the coffee was served he said, almost cheerfully, 'Now, what's all this nonsense about the curse of Tutankhamun? I thought all that was over and done with in the nineteen-twenties?'

'I take it you know the basic story,' said Ms Alexander.

'I know the basic archaeological facts,' said Dad loftily. 'Tutankhamun's tomb was discovered in the Valley of the Kings in 1922 by an English archaeologist called Howard Carter. It was hidden under a much larger tomb which had already been looted. That's how all the treasure survived so long. And when you think that Tutankhamun was a relatively minor pharaoh . . . Imagine the treasure that must have been looted from the larger tombs.'

Ms Alexander nodded. 'And what about the famous curse?'

Dad waved a hand in my direction. 'That's Matthew's department. To the best of my recollection, it amounted to little more than a string of unfortunate coincidences.'

That was typical Dad. In spite of all out experiences together, he still greeted any story involving the supernatural with obstinate unbelief. I'd always had more of an open mind on the subject – and it was getting more open all the time!

As it happened, I knew quite a bit about the curse of Tutankhamun's tomb. I'd looked it up when I knew we were coming to Egypt – just in case.

'You're talking about quite a few coincidences,' I said. 'Within just a few years, over a dozen people connected in some way with the opening of the tomb died mysteriously.'

'If you take any group of people at random, a certain number of them will die of natural causes over a period of time. Statistically speaking . . .'

You see what I mean? In spite of his paranormal experiences, Dad's still one of nature's unbelievers at heart. Ignoring the interruption, I went on with my lecture. 'Poor old Lord Carnarvon was the first to go,' I said. 'He was Howard Carter's aristocratic patron, who financed all his expeditions. When Carnarvon was in England, just before the opening of the tomb, a famous mystic called Count Hamon sent him a warning. It said death would claim him in Egypt if the tomb was opened. Carnarvon ignored the warning, went back to Egypt and attended the opening of the tomb. Next day he got bitten on the left cheek by a mosquito. The bite became infected and he died.'

'The dangers of infection in these climates are well known,' snapped Dad.

'Ah, but there's more to it than that. On the night Carnarvon died, in his Cairo hotel, there was a sudden power failure. All over Cairo, everything went black. Back home in England his faithful dog howled with grief – and died that same night! And when they opened Tutankhamun's gold coffin, there was a mark on the king's face – in exactly the same place as Carnarvon's mosquito bite.'

'Poppycock!' said Dad. 'Superstitious rumours.'

'There was another member of the expedition called Mace,' I went on. 'He was staying at the same hotel. A few days after Lord Carnarvon's death, Mace fell into a mysterious coma and died. A friend of Lord Carnarvon's called Gould visited the tomb. He died as well. Then there was Archibald Reid, the expedition's radiologist. He X-rayed Tutankhamun's mummy – some Egyptians felt that was sacrilege in itself. Anyway, Reid fell ill, went back to England and died. Richard Bethell, Lord Camarvon's secretary died of a sudden heart attack. Then Bethell's father died mysteriously . . .'

'All right, all right, Matthew,' said Dad irritably. 'Spare us the remainder of your catalogue of doom. Permit me to remind you that Howard Carter himself, the man most likely to come under the curse, lived to a healthy old age!'

I grinned. 'The exception that proves the rule!'

Ms Alexander and Jim Wainwright had both

been listening to our double act with grim amusement. 'The English and Egyptian authorities were on your father's side, Matthew,' said Ms Alexander. 'At least, until quite recently.'

'There's going to be a new Egyptian Exhibition at the British Museum,' said Jim Wainwright. 'Tutankhamun's treasure will be one of the main exhibits.'

'He won't like it!' I said, half-joking.

'Apparently he doesn't,' said Ms Alexander drily.

'You said the English and Egyptian governments used to agree with me about the curse,' said Dad. 'Do I take it they've changed their minds?'

'Let's just say they're having serious doubts,' said Wainwright.

Dad raised his eyebrows. 'Indeed? May I ask why?'

'The curse seems to have been . . . reactivated,' said Wainwright solemnly.

'The exhibition is still in the planning stage,' said Ms Alexander. 'As I'm sure you can imagine, the practical problems of transporting such a treasure are immense.'

'Not to mention the security ones,' said Jim

Wainwright. 'The stuff's ancient, a lot of it's very fragile and, to make matters worse, it's pretty well priceless.'

'Where does the curse come in?' I asked.

'A considerable number of people are involved in setting up the exhibition,' said Ms Alexander. 'Over the past few weeks, five of them have died – suddenly and mysteriously . . .'

Chapter Six

The Curse Returns

'The first victim was an Egyptian millionaire called Husani,' said Ms Alexander. 'He was one of the main sponsors of the exhibition, and offered to pay some of the costs of mounting it.'

'Just like Lord Carnarvon supporting Carter,' I said. 'What happened to him – your Egyptian millionaire, I mean.'

'He got bitten on the left cheek,' said Wainwright. 'Soon after that he died. On the night of his death there was a sudden blackout all over Cairo.'

'Was there any kind of warning?' I asked.

Wainwright nodded. 'Just before he died, Husani received a message from a prophet called Abd al' Alit. It said death would claim him if the relics of the pharaoh were disturbed yet again.'

'Very like Lord Carnarvon,' I pointed out.

There was a moment of uncomfortable silence.

'Husani's death started the panic,' said Ms Alexander. 'Some fool of a journalist wrote an article in a popular paper about the return of the curse. When more deaths followed – well, now the whole of Cairo's in an uproar about it. There's a sort of backlash building up against all Western influences. The Egyptian Government is very worried.'

'What about these other deaths?' asked Dad.

'A wealthy friend of Husani's died of a mysterious fever,' said Wainwright. 'A radiologist called Bakari, who'd been working on X-raying some of the mummies, had a sudden heart attack. Then Husani's secretary fell ill and died. The secretary's father died soon afterwards . . .'

'It's a roughly similar pattern,' I said. 'To the original deaths associated with the opening of the tomb, I mean. If the pattern continues, then there are more deaths to come.'

Ms Alexander frowned. 'What makes you say that?'

'There were about twenty people present when Tutankhamun's tomb was opened,' I said. 'At least twelve of them died afterwards.'

'But this curse idea is nonsense!' commented Dad. 'There was a Tutankhamun exhibition which toured recently without any particular trouble. Anyway, where does Rashid come into all this? And why is British Intelligence involved?'

'Rashid is the leader of an ultra-fundamentalist terrorist group,' said Ms Alexander. 'He and his followers believe that Egypt should have no contact at all with the West.'

'No technology, no bank loans, no tourists,' added Wainwright. 'And none of this Western nonsense about democracy and human rights. He wants a return to the days when Egypt was a great nation, ruled by a pharaoh.'

'Pharaoh Rashid, presumably,' I said.

'Very probably,' said Ms Alexander. 'The present Egyptian Government is keen to strengthen links with the West. There's a lot of poverty and inequality still, and the economy's not all that strong. They need all the help they can get – and Egypt desperately needs the money it gets from tourism.'

'Rashid's lot take the line that all tourists are blasphemers,' said Wainwright. 'We believe he's involved with the groups behind the recent bombings and machine-gun attacks.'

'He boasted of it to us,' I said.

'Rashid is saying that the proposed tour of the Tutankhamun Exhibition is an act of sacrilege,' Wainwright went on. 'He says the curse will fall on everyone involved with it, organisers and visitors alike.'

'Why not just cancel it?' suggested Dad.

'Because the Tutankhamun Exhibition is an important symbol of closer links between Egypt and the West,' said Ms Alexander. 'It's going to London first, then it will tour Europe, and then America, ending up in New York.'

Wainwright said, 'There'll be a whole string of opening ceremonies, each one stuffed with celebrities and VIPs, prime ministers, ministers, the lot.'

I nodded. 'And if it leaves a trail of death and destruction behind it . . .'

Dad poured himself another glass of wine. 'I'm still not sure what you expect us to do. As I told you, I'm not equipped to deal with terrorists.'

'There are two aspects to this affair,' said Ms Alexander. 'The curse of Tutankhamun – if it exists – and the way Rashid is exploiting it for his own ends. Now, with the help of the Egyptian Security Services, we can look after Rashid and his friends. But just as you're not equipped to deal with terrorists, we're not equipped to cope with the paranormal. We want you to concentrate on the curse – leave the terrorists to us!'

'The trouble is they're all mixed up,' I commented.

'We're investigating all five of the deaths,' Ms Alexander went on. 'Our problem is that they all happened before we got out here, and it's hard to backtrack. I can let you have copies of the medical reports.'

'If you please . . .' said Dad.

'Of course,' said Jim Wainwright with professional detachment, 'what we really need is a nice fresh corpse.'

'Just as long as it isn't mine or Matthew's,' replied Dad.

The gruesome subject reminded me of something. 'Tell me a bit more about your side of things,' I said. 'That agent, the one who was killed by the pyramids . . .'

'Carstairs was a specialist in infiltration,' said Ms Alexander. 'We sent him out here in advance with cover as a shady arms dealer. Terrorists always need arms. He made contact with Rashid's lot and was beginning to get closer to them. He sent a message that he was on the verge of some great discovery – and then he was killed.'

'Whatever it was must have something to do with that golden scarab,' I said. 'Let's have another look at it, Jim.'

Wainwright took the envelope out of his pocket and handed it over. I tipped out the scarab, studying it as it lay gleaming in my palm.

'I've got a feeling it's important in some way. Why was Rashid so desperate to get it back?'

'Presumably it's an important symbol of his movement,' suggested Dad.

I shook my head. 'If that was all, Carstairs wouldn't have bothered to steal it. No, it means something . . .' I looked at Wainwright. 'Can I hang on to this for a bit?'

Wainwright looked at Ms Alexander.

'You and your father are the ones Carstairs passed it to,' she said. 'Keep it by all means, if it's of any help.'

Dad frowned. 'I don't think that's a very good idea, Matthew. It's too dangerous having it in your possession.'

'As long as Rashid thinks we've got it, the danger's the same whether we actually have or not,' I pointed out. 'If the worst comes to the worst, I may be able save our necks by handing it over!'

I put the scarab back into the envelope and tucked it in an inside pocket.

Dad wasn't happy about it, but he gave in pretty ungracefully as usual. He looked at his watch. 'Well, it's been a long day. If there's nothing else for the moment?'

'There's a meeting at ten tomorrow morning at the Egyptian Museum,' said Ms Alexander. 'Everyone involved with the Tutankhamun Exhibition will be there. I think you should both attend. I'll introduce you to everyone, it'll give you some official status.'

Dad rose. 'Ten o'clock, then. Come along, Matthew.'

'Better tell me your room numbers, just in case I need to contact you,' said Wainwright.

I nodded. 'Fine. And you can give me yours.'

We exchanged room numbers, said good night and made our way to the lift.

As we sped upwards I looked at Dad. 'Another fine mess!'

'I don't like it, Matthew,' he said seriously. 'I could face investigating the paranormal because I've never been entirely sure I believed in it. Murderous fanatics with guns are all too real!'

Once in our suite we said good night to each other and went off to our respective bedrooms.

The Pyramid Incident

Tired as I was, I found I couldn't sleep. The events of the day kept whirling through my mind. I'd got the scarab under my pillow. Halfway between sleeping and waking, I got the idea it was trying to tell me something . . .

I found myself in the desert, standing before a lone pyramid amongst the dunes.

A door opened in the pyramid, sending out a blaze of light.

I moved towards the pyramid. I didn't want to go to it, but I was drawn by some unseen force.

Then I heard the metallic scratching sound . . .

It took me a moment to fully wake up and realise that the sound wasn't in my dream. It was real.

Someone was trying to open the door of the suite. Presumably they had a pass-key, but it wasn't doing them any good – I'd put the security bolt on the door before going to bed.

I jumped out of bed and then hesitated, wondering what to do.

The light went on in Dad's room and a moment later he appeared, blinking like a bad-tempered owl.

'What's happening, Matthew, why are you awake?'

'Someone's trying to get in.'

Suddenly there came a loud rapping at the door. An Arab-accented voice called, 'Professor Stirling!'

Before I could stop him, Dad called, 'Yes, who is it?'

'Hotel Security,' said the voice. 'There has been an attack on Mr Wainwright. Ms Alexander wishes you to come at once to his room.'

Dad was actually going to open the door when I grabbed his arm. 'Hold it!' I whispered fiercely.

'What's the matter?'

'You don't read enough thrillers, Dad,' I said. 'The kind where the dim heroine gets a mysterious phone-call and trots off happily to keep a rendezvous with the villain at the deserted warehouse . . .'

I went to the phone and dialled Wainwright's room. It rang – and rang and rang.

I put down the phone. 'You see?'

'But if he's hurt . . .'

'If he's hurt Ms Alexander would be with him,' I said.

The voice outside the door shouted, 'Please hurry, the matter is urgent.'

I went back to the door and called, 'Hold on. I've just called Hotel Security, they're sending some more men up to escort us.'

There was no reply. I went to the door and listened. After a moment, I thought I heard footsteps hurrying away.

I turned away from the door to find Dad glaring at me. 'Well, are you going to phone Hotel Security?'

I thought for a moment. 'No.'

'Why not? Suppose Wainwright really is hurt?'

I shook my head. 'I'm pretty sure that message was a fake. Jim's probably just out on the town. And besides, if someone came to the door and said they were from Hotel Security – how would I know if they were from Hotel Security or not?' I paused. 'And even if they were . . .'

'What?'

'Jim Wainwright said Rashid had friends everywhere, remember?'

The Unexplained

'So what do we do?'

I considered calling Ms Alexander, and decided against it. Better wait till morning.

'We don't do anything. We stay put till we speak to Wainwright or Ms Alexander in the morning, and we don't open the door till one of them comes to get us.'

'I bow to your superior literary experience, Matthew,' said Dad sarcastically. 'It's nice to think all that time reading trashy thrillers hasn't been wasted.'

Grumpily he stomped back to bed.

I went back to bed as well, and spent the rest of the night trying to sleep. I drifted off eventually and woke early a few hours later.

I grabbed the bedside phone and dialled Wainwright's number. A sleepy voice said, 'Yeah?'

'It's me, Matt,' I said.

He yawned. 'What's the time? I had a late night.'

'I had a pretty exciting night myself,' I said.

I told him what had happened the night before. 'I take it you weren't attacked and hurt,' I concluded.

'Not a bit of it. I was at a nightclub, actually, watching some first-class belly-dancing.'

'You've been seeing too many James Bond films!'

'It's actually an Egyptian art-form, Matt . . .' His voice became serious. 'You did exactly the right thing. Now listen, stay where you are till I come and get you. Don't even go down to breakfast, have it in your room. All right?'

'All right,' I said, and put down the phone.

I picked it up again and ordered two full English breakfasts from room service.

Then I went and woke up Dad, who was snoring loudly, and told him what was going on.

We were both up and dressed and hungry by the time there was a rap on the door.

A cheerful voice called, 'Room service!'

I went and opened the door.

A biggish man in the uniform of a hotel waiter pushed a laden trolley into the room.

I noticed that his jacket was a bit small for him.

'Good morning, gentlemen, lovely day!' he said cheerfully. He closed the door behind him, took a gun from his pocket and said, 'The scarab, please. At once, or I kill you both.'

Chapter Seven

Murder at the Museum

Dad and I just stood there, frozen in astonishment. I've got no excuse for my stupidity in opening the door.

Perhaps it was because it was morning, and the sun was shining. I'd talked to Jim Wainwright and I assumed the immediate crisis was over.

Perhaps it was because I was short of sleep.

Perhaps it was because I'd just ordered breakfast

myself and I was hungry, and I was expecting it to arrive . . .

'The scarab,' said the man again. 'Quickly now, or I shoot.'

It was quite obvious that he was deadly serious.

'It's in the hotel safe,' said Dad.

'You lie. We know that you took it from the safe last night. Give me the scarab or I kill the boy.'

'Give it to him, Matthew,' said Dad.

'It's in my bedroom,' I said. 'Under the pillow.'

The man gestured with his gun. 'Get it!'

I backed away towards the bedroom door and edged towards the bed. The man followed, keeping me covered with his gun.

I went to the head of my bed and picked up one of the pillows with my right hand, revealing the padded envelope underneath.

'It's in there.'

'Do you think I am a fool? Show me.'

Using my left hand I picked up the envelope by the bottom and shook it. The golden scarab dropped out and lay gleaming on the crumpled sheet.

'Give it to me.'

Dropping the empty envelope, I picked up the scarab in my left hand and held it out.

Eagerly, the gunman stepped forward to take the scarab.

I swung the pillow in my right hand at his head and dived forward in a low rugby tackle.

The gun went off and a shot rang out somewhere over my head.

My charge knocked the man off his feet but he jumped up again at once – only to be grabbed by Dad who had hurled himself upon him.

Struggling wildly, they lurched back into the sitting-room, crashed into the breakfast trolley and fell to the ground, sending bacon, eggs and coffee all over the room.

I leaned over their writhing bodies and grabbed the man's gun-hand, wrenching the automatic out of his grasp.

The big man, who seemed to be amazingly strong, threw Dad off, bounded to his feet and hurled himself towards me, ignoring the gun in my hand.

Maybe the thing had a hair-trigger, or perhaps I squeezed it too hard out of sheer nerves.

In any event, the gun went off in my hand.

The man stopped dead, clapping his hand to his ear with a yell of rage and pain.

Backing away, I pointed the gun at his head, trying to look as if I'd done it on purpose. 'The next one goes between the eyes!' I snarled.

Even then I think he might have tried to jump me and get the scarab – except that someone flung open the door to our suite.

It was Jim Wainwright, a gun in his hand.

The man sprang towards him. Instantly, Wainwright dropped him with a left uppercut to the jaw.

I drew a deep, shuddering breath and handed Wainwright the gun. 'Here, you'd better have this.'

He took it and put it in his pocket. He put his own gun away and bent over the man.

'He'll be out for a while.' He straightened up. 'I see you nicked his ear. I didn't know you were such a dead shot.'

'Neither did I, it was pure accident.'

Dad was on his feet by now, brushing himself down and straightening his glasses.

'Are you all right, Matthew?'

'More or less. You?'

He nodded and turned to Wainwright. 'How did you manage to turn up in the traditional nick of time once again?'

'I thought I'd better come and make sure you were all right. I found the real room-waiter unconscious at the end of your corridor, so it occurred to me something just might be wrong . . .'

He got on the telephone and had a short, intense conversation in Arabic. Shortly afterwards, two Egyptian policemen appeared and carted the still-unconscious gunman away.

'They may get something out of him, but I doubt it,' said Wainwright. He surveyed the scattered remains of our room-service breakfast and then turned to me. 'You've still got the scarab?'

I nodded.

'Right. Let's go down and get something to eat, shall we?'

I returned the scarab to its envelope, tucked it in an inside pocket, and we followed him from the room.

We joined Ms Alexander for breakfast in the big main dining room and brought her up to date on the night's events.

'Two attempts in one night,' she said thoughtfully. 'In a busy hotel, with police all around the area.'

'They're certainly desperate to get that scarab back,' said Wainwright. 'I wonder why.'

Ms Alexander said, 'Maybe it has some special mystical significance to them.'

I nodded. 'I think that's true. But I can't help feeling there's something else.'

'Let's have another look at it,' said Dad.

I took the envelope from my pocket and tipped the golden beetle on to the snowy-white tablecloth. We all stared down at it. I studied the lines engraved on the broad golden back, the tiny winking diamond, the two ruby-red eyes.

Dad fished in his pocket and produced a small black instrument, rather like a stopwatch. He opened it, revealing a dial, and passed it over the scarab. The needle on the dial flickered, just a little, and there was the faintest of beeps.

'Well, I can tell you one thing,' he said calmly. 'It's radioactive.'

I gave a yelp of alarm. 'What? I've been carrying that thing about in my pocket. I slept with it under my pillow. Am I going to grow another head or something?'

'Relax,' said Dad cheerfully. 'The radiation it's giving off is minimal. Less than you'd get from a granite building or a mobile phone.'

Jim Wainwright frowned. 'That's odd . . .'

'What is?' I asked.

'Radioactivity – it's cropped up somewhere recently . . .' He frowned and shook his head. 'It's no good, I can't remember where. I'll have to check the reports.' He looked at Dad. 'Inspector Mahmoud promised to bring the dossiers on all the curse-related deaths to this morning's meeting for you.'

Ms Alexander looked at her watch. 'Time we were on our way to the museum . . .'

* * *

Since our hotel and the museum were both on the Midan Tahrir, we didn't have far to go.

We were just about to go into the museum when it happened.

We heard a cheerful shout from somewhere behind us. 'Ms Alexander! Mr Wainwright! Wait for me!'

We turned and saw a plump, middle-aged man coming across the square towards us. He gave us a friendly wave.

'It's Dr Abasi, one of the assistant curators,' said Ms Alexander. 'Nice chap, very dedicated. He's been working on arrangements for the exhibition with us. He must be on his way to the meeting.'

As Dr Abasi's bustling figure hurried towards us, a black limousine swept round the corner of the square at high speed. Swerving, it smashed straight into Abasi, sending him flying through the air to land almost at our feet.

The car went hurtling round another corner and disappeared.

Dad ran to the crumpled body and kneeled to

examine it. Then he rose, shaking his head. 'Dead, I'm afraid – he's got a fractured skull. He must have been killed instantly.'

A policeman was running across the square and Wainwright went to deal with him.

I shuddered and looked away. 'They're sticking closely to the script,' I said. 'Only now they've moved closer to the present day.'

'What are you talking about?' said Ms Alexander sharply.

'The Egyptians were planning to hold a Tutankhamun exhibition in Paris, back in the early seventies,' I said. 'The man in charge had a dream, warning him he was doomed if the treasure left Egypt. He wanted to cancel the exhibition, but his bosses wouldn't listen.'

'So what happened then?' asked Ms Alexander impatiently.

'He was killed by a speeding car on the way to a meeting.'

The planning meeting was postponed out of respect

to the late Dr Abasi. The curator of the museum came down and had a brief word with us. He was a tall, distinguished-looking man with, not surprisingly, a deeply worried expression.

He shook his head sadly, as Dr Abasi's body was loaded into an ambulance. 'If this goes on we shall have to cancel the exhibition,' he said. 'If all those who work on it are doomed to die, one by one . . . Who is to undertake the work?'

'Why not put out a rumour that the exhibition really is cancelled,' suggested Ms Alexander. 'Maybe that will buy us some time to find out what's really going on.'

A police car drew up and Inspector Mahmoud got out, clutching a bundle of files.

'I have been informed of what has happened,' he said stiffly. 'Since the meeting is cancelled, I bring your consultant the promised reports.'

He handed the files over to Dad.

'Any luck with Rashid?' asked Wainwright.

Gloomily Inspector Mahmoud shook his head. 'He is nowhere to be found. My informants tell me Rashid left Cairo on an important journey. Where to, nobody knows. The revolutionary elements in Cairo are in a state of great excitement. There are rumours that something enormously important is to happen soon. There is to be a sign . . . A Great One is to appear!' He sighed. 'Once again, nobody knows exactly what is going on!'

'Well, keep looking,' said Wainwright. 'And good luck!'

'There is one thing more, Mr Wainwright,' Mahmoud said. 'You remember the man who was killed at the Giza Pyramids?' He gave Dad and me a satirical look. 'The death at which your two consultants here were definitely not present?'

'What about it?'

Mahmoud took a crumpled piece of tissue paper from his pocket. 'The dead man's pockets had been rifled, but this was found in his shoe. It appears to be in some kind of code. Perhaps you can make something of it.'

Wainwright took the piece of paper which seemed to be covered with figures and symbols. 'I'll see what

I can do,' he said casually.

I had a feeling he was trying not to look too eager.

We went back to the hotel for a meeting, held in Ms Alexander's suite, which was even bigger and more luxurious than our own. Taxpayers' money, I suppose.

We sat around a highly polished table in a sumptuously furnished sitting-room and sipped coffee.

Dad was ploughing his way through a pile of death reports.

Jim Wainwright was busy decoding the message found in the dead agent's pocket.

I had put the golden scarab on the table before me and was staring gloomily at it.

Ms Alexander was quietly seething. 'Well!' she snapped. 'Somebody say something! We must have *some* ideas between us.'

Dad looked up from the pile of post-mortem reports. 'None of this is much help. So far all these deaths seem – ambiguous.'

'What's that supposed to mean?'

He shrugged. 'Heart attacks, mysterious fevers

and infections – all apparently natural deaths. But the victims *could* all have been murdered. All these natural deaths could have been faked.'

'You're sure of that?'

Dad gave her a sinister smile. 'Given reasonable laboratory facilities, I could soon whip you up a killer toxin myself. A dab on the end of something sharp – then a quick pin-prick, followed by fever and death . . .'

Wainwright looked up from his decoding. 'There are lots of ways you can cause a seemingly natural death. The Russians had a line in gas-lighters in the bad old Cold War days. Snap one under the victim's nose – instant heart attack!'

'And Rashid's an experienced terrorist,' said Ms Alexander thoughtfully. 'He'd have access to the technology, or he'd know someone who'd know someone.' She sighed. 'So we can't tell for sure if all these people were deliberately killed or just victims of Tutankhamun's curse!'

'They were murdered,' I said savagely. 'I'm convinced of it. Every single one of them was deliberately killed.'

Chapter Eight

The Pyramid
of Power

Ms Alexander gave me an astonished look.

'How can you be so sure?'

'Because it all feels scripted – arranged somehow. Look at this last death!'

'What about it?'

I struggled to explain why I felt so certain. 'The paranormal isn't so precise. And that's just not how curses work. They're general, not specific. They bring ill fortune, they say you'll come to a bad end.

They don't guarantee that you'll die in exactly the same way as somebody doing the same job over thirty years ago!'

I paused. 'What's more, that earlier death was a genuine traffic accident – whether the curse caused it or not. What happened today was a deliberate killing. The car swerved towards him, I saw it.'

'What about the first death?' objected Dad. 'That Egyptian millionaire. The mark on the left cheek in the same place as Lord Carnarvon – and Tutankhamun. The blackout in Cairo on the night of his death . . .'

'That was the most obvious fake of all,' I said, sounding a lot more confident than I felt.

Dad frowned. 'Why do you say that?'

'It's all so . . . so stagey, so over-elaborate. That poor old millionaire, Husani, hadn't opened any tombs, that all happened nearly ninety years ago. All right, so he supported the exhibition and maybe that offended Tutankhamun. Maybe he *was* doomed. But why should the curse take the trouble to kill him in exactly the same way as Lord Carnarvon?'

'So how did he die?' said Dad triumphantly. 'How

did Rashid manage the sting on the left cheek? Tell me that!'

I thought hard for a moment. Suddenly inspiration struck. 'Blowpipe!' I said airily.

'You're not serious!'

'Perfectly serious,' I said. 'A blowpipe and a poison dart.'

Jim Wainwright looked up again. 'Matthew could be right,' he said seriously. 'Victim feels a sharp pain in the cheek, thinks he's been stung, brushes the dart away . . . Then he sickens and dies. It's a very common weapon in some parts of Africa – and Egypt's still Africa after all.'

Dad still didn't seem to be convinced. 'And what about the blackout over Cairo? Exactly the same as when Lord Carnarvon died!'

'Oh come on, Dad,' I said. 'Simple sabotage at the power station. Child's play for someone like Rashid.'

Suddenly I burst out laughing. Here I was, pushing the rational explanation – with Dad holding out for the paranormal!

Dad looked offended. 'What's so funny?'

'I was just thinking,' I said. 'Who's supposed to be the believer and who's the sceptic round here?'

'I was just playing devil's advocate,' said Dad with an air of offended dignity. 'Testing out your ideas by questioning them.' Suddenly he smiled. 'And I must say, Matthew, I'm convinced. I think you're absolutely right.'

Ms Alexander hammered her fist on the table. 'And so do I. For one thing, it seems to be the only theory we've got. So, we forget the curse . . .'

'That's right,' I said. 'You just concentrate on getting your hands on Rashid. Put him away and the deaths will stop.'

'It's not that easy,' she said gloomily. 'Mahmoud's a dry old stick but he's a first-class policeman – and he knows every back alleyway in Cairo. If he can't find Rashid . . .'

'Maybe we could try to work out the next likely victim,' suggested Dad. 'You could set a trap.'

Ms Alexander didn't look keen. 'How could we be sure we'd chosen the right one? And if we were wrong, somebody else might get killed.'

'Besides, Inspector Mahmoud said Rashid had left Cairo,' I reminded her. 'Gone on some important journey.'

She nodded. 'If we knew where he'd gone . . .'

'I may be able to help,' said Wainwright. He tapped the sheet of thin paper he'd been working on.

'What is that thing anyway?' I asked.

'These are poor Carstairs's last notes – written in one of the standard department codes.' Wainwright's face was grim. 'Notes for a report he never lived to write.'

Ms Alexander had no time for sentiment. 'What do they say?' she asked. 'Anything useful?'

'It's all a bit scrappy. He seems convinced that Rashid was planning some kind of revolution. Presumably that's why he's getting everyone stirred up about the curse . . . There's something about Rashid going to the Pyramid of Power.' He looked up. 'It's the last bit that baffles me. It goes, "I have stolen their precious scarab and they are after me . . . The scarab shows the way and opens the door . . ."'

I stared down at the golden beetle on the table

before me. '"The scarab shows the way . . ." How?'

I looked round the room for inspiration. There wasn't much to be had. Pictures of tourist attractions, a framed map of Egypt . . .

I looked at the beetle . . . and back at the map.

I glanced at the map again – and studied the lines on the beetle's back.

'Got it!' I said. 'The lines are a map of Egypt. This central line is the Nile . . . I looked up at the others. 'And I'll bet the place where this little diamond is set is the Pyramid of Power!'

It was Jim Wainwright who worked it out for us. All that SAS training, I expect.

He got hold of a proper map and a magnifying glass and checked it all out. Once you had worked out that the central line on the scarab's back was the Nile, it was pretty easy to identify the various dots. They represented Cairo in the north, Luxor in the south, Al-Minyah to the west and Hurghada to the east.

Wainwright bent over the map with a pencil and ruler.

The Pyramid Incident

'If we draw a line between Cairo and Luxor, and another between Al-Minyah and Hurghada, they intersect here . . . which approximates the place where the diamond is set on the scarab's back . . .'

'And where's here?' demanded Ms Alexander.

'Somewhere in the Eastern Desert,' said Wainwright. He peered at the map. 'Eight kilometres south of an oasis called Gabal Gayasi . . .'

Suddenly he broke off. 'That's it!'

'What's what?' I asked.

'Radioactivity!' said Wainwright. 'I remember now! There was a story in *Al-Ahram*, the Cairo newspaper, the day we arrived. A man staggered into Gabal Gayasi oasis, terribly burned. He died next day. He just about managed to tell them his name, and to mutter something about a burning pyramid. Apparently his name was Zaki – he was a well-known tomb-robber. What puzzled the police was that there are no tombs and no pyramids in that part of the desert. They were even more puzzled when they shipped the body back to Cairo for a post-mortem and discovered it was radioactive.'

We all looked at each other.

If the Pyramid of Power was anywhere, this had to be the place. It was our chance to find Rashid and trap him.

'Well,' I said, 'Gabal Gayasi here we come!'

It was night-time and we were bouncing across the desert, threading our way between towering sand dunes in a big Land Rover. We'd been travelling all day and for much of the night.

Wainwright was driving with Ms Alexander up front, navigating beside him. Behind us was another identical Land Rover, filled with tough-looking Arabs, all armed to the teeth.

Jim Wainwright had produced them from somewhere, saying vaguely that they were 'local operatives'. It was pretty clear that they were mercenaries, loyal to whoever paid them.

After much discussion, we had decided against involving the police. For one thing, we weren't sure they'd go along with our theory. For another, there was a definite danger that Rashid had friends in the official world – friends who might warn him we were coming.

'You know, Matthew,' said Dad quietly, 'nasty and dangerous as it is, this affair does have one redeeming feature.'

'What's that?'

'There's nothing paranormal involved.'

'Don't be too sure,' I said. 'It's not over yet!'

'Come now, Matthew,' said Dad. 'You demonstrated yourself that all our problems are due to simple human villainy. I can't tell you what a relief it is not to have any dealings with your alien friends!'

We've had one or two close encounters ourselves during our adventures, but Dad's never cared for it. He hates it when he sees things he doesn't want to believe in.

'Well, you never know,' I persisted. 'Lots of people believe that ancient Egypt could never have reached such a high level of science, or even built the pyramids, without the help of visitors from the stars.'

'There's no scientific proof . . .'

'The Egyptians themselves believed that their

pharaohs were immortal,' I went on. 'And what about the pyramid shape itself?'

'What about it?'

'It's got extraordinary powers. Food placed inside a model pyramid stays preserved for ages. And if you put blunt razor-blades inside, they actually get sharper!'

Dad sniffed scornfully, and made no reply.

As we travelled on through the desert, I had a sudden strange conviction that he was wrong, that somehow alien forces were involved.

I waited almost eagerly to see what would happen.

In the front seat, Ms Alexander peered at the map. 'We must be nearly there by now. It's eight kilometres since the oasis.'

I looked out of the window. 'Can't see any pyramids,' I said. 'Just sand dunes.'

There was the sudden stutter of a machine gun. A line of bullets kicked up sand just before our wheels.

Wainwright stood on the brakes and we slid to a halt. The Land Rover behind us did the same.

The Pyramid Incident

Black-robed men lined the tops of the sand dunes all around us. They carried rifles and submachine guns.

'Bedouin,' said Wainwright. 'Wild desert tribesmen.'

The black-robed men stood motionless on their sand dunes. Then one of them broke off from the rest and walked down towards us.

It was Rashid.

'Welcome,' he said. He walked to the Land Rover behind us and snarled something in Arabic.

The second Land Rover started up again, wheeled round in a big circle, and headed back the way we had come.

We had just lost our mercenary army.

Rashid came back up to us.

'I told them they would be unharmed if they left at once,' he said.

'Very generous of you,' said Wainwright.

'I have no wish to kill fellow Egyptians,' said Rashid. 'You others, of course, are a different matter. Get out, all of you.'

We got out.

Rashid looked around our little group and then

fixed on me. 'The scarab,' he said.

Somehow he knew that I was the one who carried it.

I took it out of my pocket and handed it to him.

He stared at it eagerly, then closed his hand tightly around it.

'Why is it so important to you?' I asked. 'You must have solved the secret of the map before you lost the scarab or you wouldn't be here.'

Rashid's reply recalled the last message of the man he'd murdered. 'The scarab shows the way *and* opens the door . . .'

He stared greedily at the scarab in his hand. 'Come,' he said, 'you shall see the great power you have blasphemed against. You shall see my incarnation as a pharaoh. And it will be the last thing you ever see.'

He called out a command in Arabic and turned to the others. 'Stay here. If you move or speak, you will die.'

Dad opened his mouth to protest, and I could see Wainwright was poised to spring.

The Pyramid Incident

'Please, do as he says,' I said. 'It's all right.'

Strangely enough, I wasn't in the least afraid. I felt more curious than anything else. And I had the strange, almost dreamy feeling that things were moving towards a predestined conclusion.

Leaving Dad and the others under guard, I followed Rashid between the dunes, across a stretch of open desert, and up to the foot of a tall sand dune that stood isolated from the rest.

Rashid held up the scarab and began chanting in Arabic.

The golden beetle glowed with unearthly light.

The sands of the tall dune before me began sifting away, flowing away like water to reveal the shape of a glowing pyramid.

Rashid bowed low before it.

A door opened in the side of the pyramid facing us, letting out a blaze of light.

Rashid resumed his chanting but I wasn't listening. I felt the touch of an alien mind, just like I had felt before in the Australian desert.

Perhaps that earlier communication made this one

easier. Somehow I knew that the alien in the pyramid was aware of me. That it was . . . curious.

I tried to communicate, not in words but in feelings and images. I summoned up all I knew of Egypt, its glorious past, the years of poverty and suffering, the hopeful future.

I focused on Rashid, on his cruelty and ambition and his lust for absolute power. I summoned up those he had killed, or had caused to die. I thought of those who had been killed for working on the exhibition, and of the deaths I had actually seen.

I thought of the man in the crumpled white suit collapsing before the Sphinx.

I saw the friendly curator flying through the air in front of his museum and falling dead at my feet.

Then I waited.

Rashid's chant rose to a climax and he strode confidently towards the blazing doorway.

I knew without being told what he expected – that the power of the pyramid would make him superhuman, immortal . . . A pharaoh!

A tongue of flame suddenly streaked out from the

doorway and Rashid became a pillar of fire.

For a moment he whirled and spun, screaming. Then he vanished, reduced to a sprinkling of fine ashes in the sands.

The ashes blew away.

The door in the pyramid closed.

I waited.

From somewhere behind or below the pyramid there appeared a glowing disc. It rose silently upwards, streaked across the night sky and disappeared.

Whatever alien being inhabited the pyramid, it was going home.

I turned and walked away.

When I reached the edge of the dunes I turned and looked back at the pyramid. For a moment it remained, glowing against the night sky.

Then, with a thunderous roar, it exploded, disappearing in a towering column of flame.

I turned and ran back to the Land Rover.

There was no sign of the ring of black-robed, armed men on the surrounding sand dunes. They had vanished into the desert.

Dad and Wainwright and Ms Alexander were still standing there, exactly as I had last seen them. They looked dazed, staring towards the spot where the pyramid had vanished. They seemed to be suffering from some kind of psychic shock.

'Hey, wake up!' I yelled. 'I'm back!'

Slowly they came back to life.

'Matthew, are you all right?' said Dad. 'I thought . . .' His voice tailed off.

Ms Alexander seemed to recover her full senses first. 'What happened?' she demanded. 'Rashid, those men . . .'

I took a deep breath and began.

Next morning we met with Ms Alexander and Wainwright and went through the events in detail. They decided it was best to put out an official cover story.

We had discovered that Rashid had faked the deaths apparently caused by Tutankhamun's curse to stir up superstitious fear in the populace and pave the way for revolt.

Which was true enough, of course.

After that, according to the official story, we had tracked him to the desert, there had been some kind of fight, and a stray shot had blown up Rashid's secret arms dump.

End of story.

Now the preparations for the Tutankhamun Exhibition could go ahead.

Ms Alexander and Jim Wainwright thanked us warmly for all our help, and went off to get things underway.

Dad and I got ourselves seats on the next plane home.

As we waited in the departure lounge Dad said quietly, 'So you believe I was wrong, Matthew? You believe alien influences were involved after all.'

I shrugged. 'Possibly. Perhaps the Ancient Egyptians did have visitors from space. Maybe the aliens ruled them for a time, or gave the pharaohs superhuman powers. When they departed they left someone, or something, behind. Rashid found out about it, tried to misuse its power and was punished.'

'And the whatever-it-was has gone home?'

'Apparently,' I said. 'Maybe it decided the Egyptians didn't need it any more. Or maybe even aliens get homesick.'

'Just like us,' said Dad.

'Just like us,' I agreed. 'Can't wait for some nice English rain.'

They called our flight and we headed for the departure gate.

THE
TRANSYLVANIAN
INCIDENT

TERRANCE DICKS

Matt and Professor Stirling, the famous
paranormal investigator, are asked to go to Romania,
where blood-drained corpses are being found in a
remote region known as Transylvania.

The professor is sure it must be a
village feud, but as more eerie events unfold, can
he really remain unconvinced of Matt's theory
that a more ancient evil returned?

Turn over to read the beginning of
The Transylvanian Incident

Coming soon:
The Transylvanian Incident

Read on for a sneak preview of
Matt's next exciting adventure . . .

It was, thought the village policeman, a hell of a night.

He poked the iron stove that stood in the centre of the little room. With its whitewashed stone walls, heavy wooden table and rickety chairs, the police station was a simple enough place – and it was a lot better than the dark and stormy night outside, with its icy howling wind.

He ate the last of his sausage, swigged the last of the rough red wine and looked at the Russian-made steel watch on his wrist.

Midnight, time for his last patrol. After that, thank goodness, he could bundle himself up in his blankets and sleep till dawn.

Wrapping himself in his heavy overcoat and pulling down his cap, he went out into the darkness. As soon as he stepped out of the doorway he was buffeted by the icy wind that raced down from the mountains.

The little police station stood at the bottom of the main village street. Bracing himself, the policeman began the ascent to the main square at the top. If the village inn hadn't locked its doors yet, he might be able to cadge another glass of wine.

Head down against the wind, he began the long, steep climb. There was a full moon, and the cobbled street was bathed in its eerie light. Occasionally, black storm clouds passed across the moon, and there was a moment or two of pitch-black darkness, until the clouds passed over and the moonlight returned.

It was in one of these intervals of darkness that the policeman heard the choking scream.

It came from one of the narrow side streets, the ones on his right that ran down towards the river.

The policeman hesitated, tempted to ignore the sound. Perhaps mountain bandits had come down to rob some unfortunate shopkeeper, it happened sometimes. Ferocious, murderous types, these bandits. Armed to the teeth, they travelled in packs like wolves and had no respect for the forces of the law.

Safer not to hear anything.

On the other hand, the district police commandant was even more terrifying than the bandits.

If the commandant heard that some crime had been committed on the constable's patrol, and he'd heard nothing, done nothing . . .

Fumbling to get his heavy revolver from its holster, the policeman set off down the narrow sidestreet.

'Who's there?' he shouted in a quavering voice. 'Stay where you are; this is the police!'

The only answer was a low, blood-curdling growl.

'Halt!' screamed the policeman.

Suddenly the moonlight returned, illuminating a horrifying scene.

A sprawled shape lay on the cobbles some way ahead of him. Crouched over it was another shape, black-cloaked, its head buried in its victim's neck in a ghastly embrace.

The constable's blood turned to ice as age-old terror flooded through him.

'*Strigoi!*' he whispered.

His finger tightened on the trigger in pure terror, and the shot sounded incredibly loud in the heavy silence, its echoes reverberating around the ancient buildings.

The crouching form raised a white face, its lips bedabbled with blood. It sprang to its feet, the policeman fired again – and there was darkness as the moon vanished behind black clouds.

The darkness lasted only a few seconds, but when the moonlight returned the crouching shape was gone.

The sprawled shape on the cobbles remained.

Resisting the impulse to flee, the policeman stumbled towards the body. It lay face upwards in the moonlight, horn-rimmed glasses askew on the white face, one of the lenses smashed. There was a bloody wound in the neck, just under the jawline.

The dead man wore a tweed suit and an overcoat, well-cut clothes quite unlike those of the local peasants. To his horror the policeman recognised him. He was a foreigner, the solitary tourist staying at the village inn.

This means trouble, big trouble, thought the terrified policeman. The death of a villager, especially from such a cause, might be hushed up without too much fuss. But a foreigner . . .

Suddenly the darkness returned.

Something flapped out of the blackness, hitting the policeman in the face. Claws raked across his cheek and then the thing disappeared into the night with a whirring of leathery wings.

The constable's shaky nerve broke and he turned and fled.

Lights began to go on here and there in the village street – but no one ventured out into the night.

If you've enjoyed the mystery of *The Unexplained*, try being the sleuth yourself with:

SAXBY SMART
PRIVATE DETECTIVE

Crack all the cases!

In each story Saxby Smart – schoolboy detective – gives you, the reader, clues which help solve the mystery. Are you 'smart' enough to find the answers?

1 – *The Curse of the Ancient Mask*
A mysterious curse, suspicious sabotage of a school competition, and a very unpleasant relative all conspire to puzzle Saxby Smart, schoolboy private detective.
Stories include: *The Curse of the Ancient Mask*, *The Mark of the Purple Homework* and *The Clasp of Doom*

2 – *The Fangs of the Dragon*
A string of break-ins where nothing is stolen, a rare comic book snatched from an undamaged safe, and clues apparently leading to a hidden treasure – Saxby solves three more challenging crimes.
Stories include: *The Fangs of the Dragon*, *The Tomb of Death* and *The Treasure of Dead Man's Lane*.

3 – *The Pirate's Blood*

A bloody handprint inside a museum case containing pirate treasure, a classmate with a mysterious secret, and a strange case of arson in a bookshop require Saxby's expert help.

Stories include: *The Pirate's Blood*, *The Mystery of Mary Rogers* and *The Lunchbox of Notre Dame*.

4 – *The Hangman's Lair*

A terrifying visit to the Hangman's Lair to recover stolen money, a serious threat of blackmail, and a mystery surrounding a stranger's unearthly powers test Saxby to the limit in this set of case files!

Stories include: *The Hangman's Lair*, *Diary of Fear* and *Whispers from the Dead*.

5 – *The Eye of the Serpent*

A valuable work of art vanishes into thin air, a notorious crook returns from the dead, and there's an eerie case of stolen identity . . . Time to call in Saxby Smart!

Stories include: *The Eye of the Serpent*, *The Ghost at the Window*, *The Stranger in the Mirror*.

6 – *Five Seconds to Doomsday*

Saxby's arch enemy plots his ultimate revenge, video games vanish off a truck, and the school office is the target of an apparently pointless robbery. What's really going on?

Stories include: *Five Seconds to Doomsday*, *March of the Zombies* and *The Shattered Box*.

☆

www.piccadillypress.co.uk

☆ The latest news on forthcoming books

☆ Chapter previews

☆ Author biographies

☆ Fun quizzes

☆ Reader reviews

☆ Competitions and fab prizes

☆ Book features and cool downloads

☆ And much, much more . . .

Log on and check it out!

Piccadilly Press

☆